"Mom," asked Paulette, "will you read me this story about space travel before I go to bed?"

"I am happy to read to you," said her mom. "Sit here with me, will you?"

"Look, Mom," said
Paulette, pointing to
the book. "Is this
really a monkey in
a space ship?"

"Yes, it is," said her mom.
"The author says that the
first astronaut was
a monkey."

"How can a monkey
go into space?" asked
Paulette.
"Let's read the story
and see," said her mom.

"Wow!" said Paulette when her mom finished reading. "The first astronaut really was a monkey."

"I want to be an
astronaut, too,"
Paulette said. "I want
to be launched into
space in a flying saucer."

"Paulette," said her mom, with a smile, "the monkey went into space in a rocket, not in a flying saucer."

"All right, then I will fly
in a rocket," said
Paulette. "But I will pack
a lunch before I go."

"I will take a bamboo
sandwich and some
applesauce," said Paulette.
"That will keep me well
fed until I get home
for dinner."

"Let's talk about this
in the morning, dear,"
said Paulette's mom.
"Right now, it is time
for you to brush your
teeth and get to sleep."

Paulette brushed her
teeth at the faucet.

Then Paulette got into
bed. Her mom kissed
her good night.

Paulette wondered
about the launch.
It was a hot August
night, and she saw lots
of stars twinkling high
in the sky.

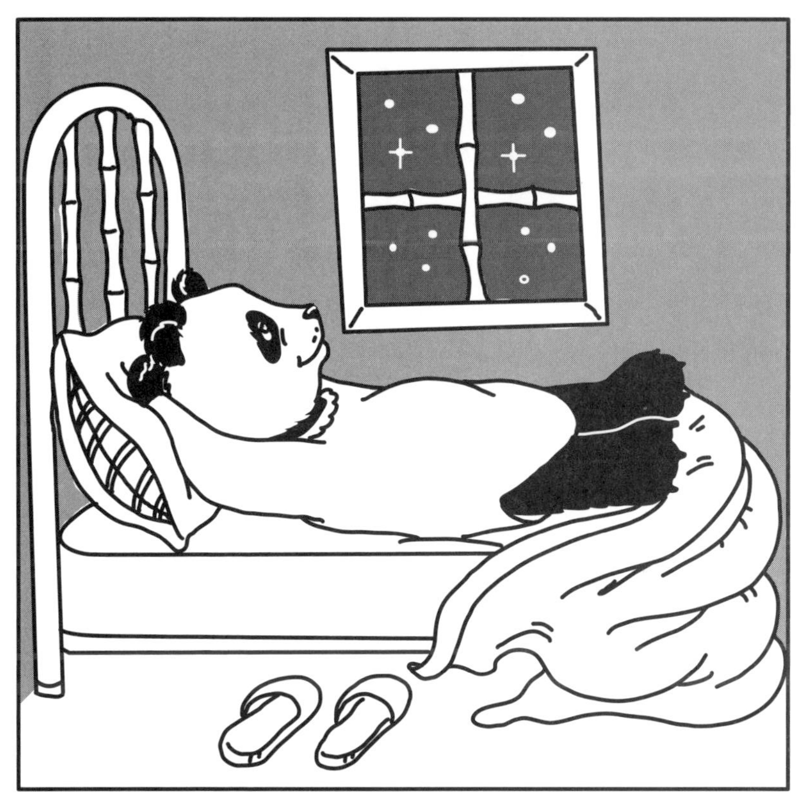

Paulette wondered if stars twinkle up in space. She kicked off her blanket. Then she yawned and stretched out on her bed.

Then Paulette fell right
to sleep.